Library of Congress Cataloging-in-Publication Data is available.

ISBN 0-590-44785-8

12 11 10 9 8 7 6 5 4 3 2 1   2 3 4 5 6 7/9
Printed in the U.S.A.   24

First Scholastic printing, August 1992

OLLIE
Goes to School

by Elizabeth B. Rodger

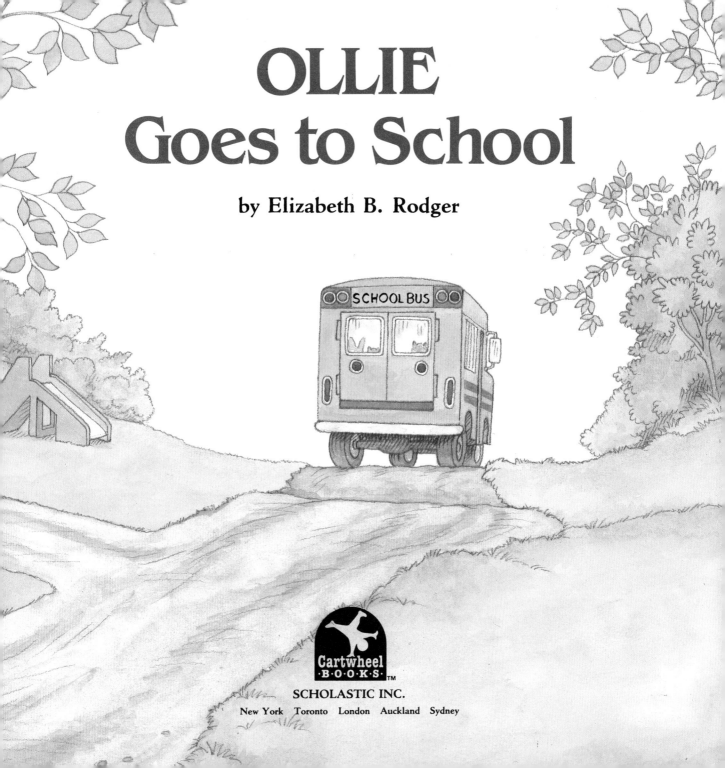

Cartwheel
·B·O·O·K·S·™

SCHOLASTIC INC.
New York Toronto London Auckland Sydney

Summer was almost over. Father Mole was chopping logs for the fires he would build on the cooler days ahead. Ellie, Dudley, and even little Ollie helped by stacking the logs in a neat pile.

"All done for today," said Father Mole.
"Hooray!" said Dudley.
"Let's tell Mother!" said Ollie.

Mother Mole was very busy.

"What are you doing?" Ellie asked.

"I'm making new overalls for Ollie to wear on his first day of school," said Mother Mole.

"What?" said Ollie. "But I don't go to school."

"You will tomorrow," said Mother Mole.

Ollie was worried. "Can I go to school if I can't read and write yet?" he asked.

"Of course," said Mother Mole. "You'll learn those things at school. But not at first. At first you will play with other children."

At suppertime, Ollie was still worried. "Will I know anyone there?"

"Not at first," said Father Mole. "But soon you will make many wonderful friends."

"What will I play with at school?" Ollie asked at
bathtime. "I won't have my toys there."

"You'll find plenty of toys at school," said Mother Mole.
"But you may take one toy with you if you like.
Why don't you take Freddie?"

"What if I get hungry or thirsty?" Ollie asked.
"Your teacher will give you something to eat and drink at snacktime," said Mother Mole.

At bedtime, Ollie gave his father a big hug.
"I'll miss Mommy while I'm at school," he said.
"She'll miss you, too," said Father Mole.

"Good night," said Father Mole.

Ollie cuddled next to Freddie. "Tomorrow is our first day of school. I think everything's going to be all right," Ollie said to him.

The next morning, holding on tightly to Freddie's waist and even more tightly to his mother's hand, Ollie was on his way to school.

Ollie's teacher was Miss Purtie. She showed Ollie a cubby that was just for him.

"This is where you will put your things," said Miss Purtie.

A name tag was hanging in Ollie's cubby. Mother Mole helped Ollie put it on.

Ollie looked around the room. There were so many children! Ollie wondered if any of them would ever want to be his friend.

Ollie clutched his mother's skirt. He didn't want her to leave.

Miss Purtie came back to talk to Ollie. "What's your friend's name?" she asked. Ollie whispered Freddie's name.

"I don't have a chair that is small enough for Freddie," Miss Purtie said. "Would you like to make one?"

"Yes," said Ollie.

That sounded like fun. So Ollie let go of his mother's skirt and gave her a good-bye hug.

Miss Purtie gave Ollie some clay, and he went to work at once.

The chair Ollie made was just the right size.

Ollie put Freddie and the little chair on the top shelf of his cubby. Freddie looked very happy.

"Would you like to play with us?" said a voice behind Ollie.

Pippy Mouse and Horton Toad were sitting next to a big box of building blocks.

"All right," Ollie said shyly.

Together, the children built a town of tall towers, short towers, fat buildings, and skinny buildings.

Then Ollie and his new friends looked at a picture book. Ollie felt very important as he held the book and turned the pages.

At snacktime the three friends sipped apple juice and shared cookies.

When Ollie glanced at his cubby, Freddie still looked very happy. Ollie was feeling good, too.

Miss Purtie took the class outside.
Ollie and his new friends rushed
to the merry-go-round. Bert Pig and
Ella Beaver offered to push.
Everyone squealed and laughed as they
whizzed around and around.

When the class returned to their room, Ollie painted a picture of Freddie.

"What a beautiful, happy picture," said Miss Purtie. "May I hang it on the wall?"

Ollie felt proud as everyone admired his work.

Then the children sat in a circle and listened to Miss Purtie read a story.

All of a sudden, the parents arrived.
Mother Mole appeared at the door. School
was over for the day.

Ollie was so busy telling Mother about
his wonderful day, he quite forgot to wave
good-bye to his new friends.

The next morning Ollie was the first to
get dressed . . . and the first to come
rushing downstairs for breakfast.

"You don't have to take me to school today," Ollie announced to his mother. "I'm going to take the bus."

Ollie was the first out the door to wait for the big yellow bus.

"Ollie, wait! You forgot Freddie," Mother Mole called.

"Oh, Mother! Freddie is too little to go to school," said Ollie. "School is for big children.

"Big children like me!"